WHEN YOUR FRIEND IS ANGRY

BY ALLAN MOREY

BLUE OWL
BOOKS

TIPS FOR CAREGIVERS

Social and emotional learning (SEL) helps children grow their self and social awareness. They will learn how to manage their emotions and foster empathy toward others. Lessons and support in SEL help children build relationship skills, establish positive habits in communication and cooperation, and make better decisions. By incorporating SEL in early reading, children will have the opportunity to explore different emotions, as well as learn ways to cope with theirs and those of others.

BEFORE READING

Explain to the reader that anger is an emotion everyone experiences.

Discuss: What causes you to become angry? How do you feel when you are mad? How do you act? Do you notice other people acting the same way?

AFTER READING

Talk to the reader about how to recognize when someone else is angry.

Discuss: How should you approach a friend who is angry? What should you do or say? How can you help a friend who is upset?

SEL GOAL

Young students struggle to understand their own emotions, and it's even more difficult for them to recognize how someone else is feeling. Being able to spot clues in a friend's body language and actions will help improve their social awareness skills. Lead a discussion about how students feel when angry and what helps calm them down. This will help students learn how to approach and communicate with a friend who might be feeling upset.

TABLE OF CONTENTS

CHAPTER 1

RECOGNIZING ANGER

What does an angry face look like? We **glare**. Our eyes narrow. When angry, our nostrils **flare**. We might wrinkle our noses. Our lips tighten and get thinner.

We also see anger in **body language**. These are movements people make that show how they feel. When angry, Emma **clenches** her jaw and balls her hands into fists.

Drew shouts and yells when he is angry. Another friend might stomp her feet or **pace**. Others shake their arms.

How do you **react** when you are angry? How have you seen your peers or friends react?

Liz said something hurtful because she was angry. She did not mean to be unkind. She was frustrated. Anger can cause people to lash out. People sometimes have a hard time understanding their feelings of anger.

MIXED SIGNALS

Different **emotions** can look similar. A friend might frown when sad. He or she could also frown when angry. Shouting or yelling could mean anger or fear. Look for more than one sign to understand what someone is feeling.

CHAPTER 2

UNDERSTANDING ANGER

We all get angry for different reasons. It can be hard to understand why someone else is mad. Think about how you feel when you are angry. That can help you understand others' feelings.

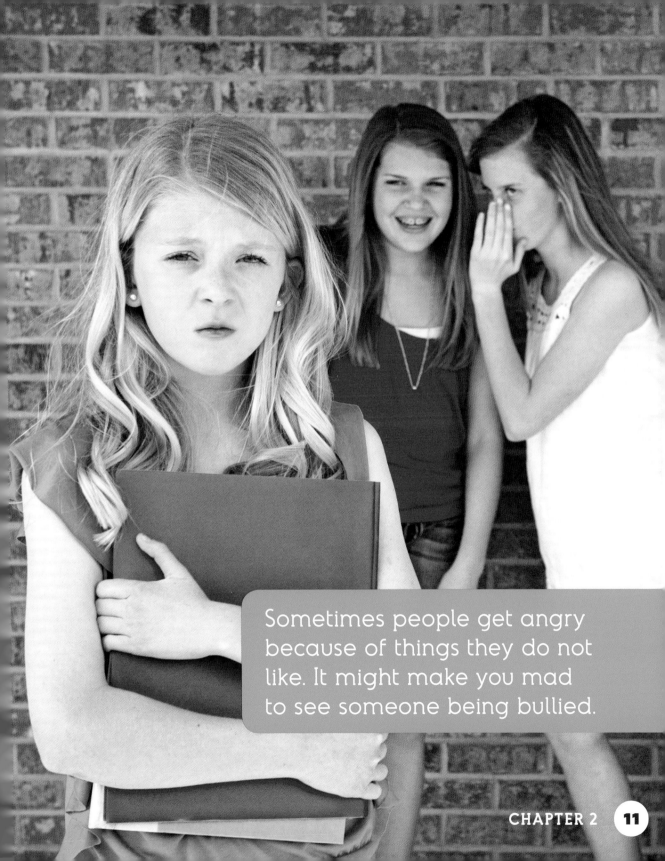

Sometimes people get angry because of things they do not like. It might make you mad to see someone being bullied.

Other times, people get angry with themselves. Why? They feel they made a mistake. A friend might be angry after breaking something. Or she might be mad after losing a game.

POSITIVE SIDE OF ANGER

Anger can be positive! It tells us something is bothering us. Getting angry shows that we care. Anger can also **motivate** us. It can make us try harder after we make a mistake.

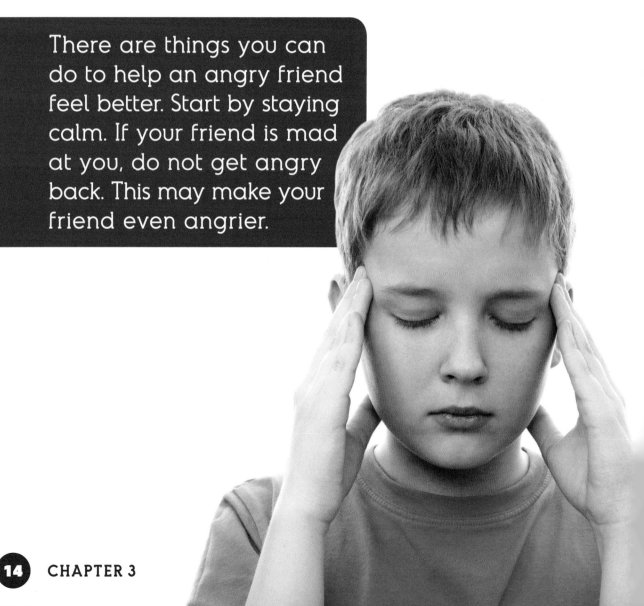

CHAPTER 3

RESPONDING TO ANGER

There are things you can do to help an angry friend feel better. Start by staying calm. If your friend is mad at you, do not get angry back. This may make your friend even angrier.

Jo asks Hope why she is angry. Then she listens. She lets Hope talk about her feelings. She doesn't interrupt, and she doesn't tell Hope to calm down. Letting her speak about her feelings helps Hope calm down.

Nate wants to be alone when he is angry. That is OK. He needs space to calm down. He will talk later, after he has calmed down.

ANGER VS. HOSTILITY

Being angry is not the same as being hostile. If someone is mad, they are upset. That is OK. To be hostile is to want to cause harm when angry. A hostile person might hurt someone or break something. That is not OK.

Nell made Meg mad. Nell doesn't try to **defend** her side. She doesn't **argue** about who was right or wrong. She apologizes. This helps Meg calm down.

Tell your friend you understand why he is angry. You don't have to agree with his reason. But **accept** his feelings. Then ask if he wants help with what upset him. Maybe you can find a **solution** together.

Helping a friend who was angry feels good. It helps you understand your friend. You can become better friends!

GOALS AND TOOLS

GROW WITH GOALS

Everyone gets angry for different reasons. Recognizing how you feel when angry will help you understand friends when they are mad.

Goal: Draw a picture of a face. Then draw the same face but show it as angry. Note the differences.

Goal: Write about a time you were angry. What made you mad? Did someone help you calm down? What did they do to help you?

Goal: Think about times you have seen friends angry. Are there ways you could have helped them?

WRITING REFLECTION

Look into a mirror and make an angry face.

1. What about your facial expression changed?

2. Make a list of things that you have felt angry about.

3. Do you feel you had a reason to be angry? Why or why not?

GLOSSARY

accept
To agree that something is correct, satisfactory, or enough.

argue
To disagree in talking about or discussing something.

body language
The gestures, movements, and mannerisms by which people communicate with others.

clenches
Closes or holds tightly.

defend
To give the reasons for something.

emotions
Feelings, such as happiness, anger, or sadness.

flare
To widen, as in a person's nostrils.

glare
To look at someone in an angry way.

motivate
To encourage someone to do something or want to do better.

pace
To walk back and forth.

react
To behave in a particular way as a response to something that has happened.

solution
An answer or means to solving a problem.

TO LEARN MORE

FACT SURFER

Finding more information is as easy as 1, 2, 3.

1. Go to www.factsurfer.com

2. Enter "**whenyourfriendisangry**" into the search box.

3. Choose your cover to see a list of websites.

INDEX

Blue Owl Books are published by Jump!, 5357 Penn Avenue South, Minneapolis, MN 55419, www.jumplibrary.com

Copyright © 2020 Jump! International copyright reserved in all countries. No part of this book may be reproduced in any form without written permission from the publisher.

Library of Congress Cataloging-in-Publication Data

Names: Morey, Allan, author.
Title: When your friend is angry / by Allan Morey.
Description: Blue owl books. | Minneapolis, MN: Jump!, Inc., [2020]
Series: You've got a friend | Includes index. | Audience: Ages 7–10.
Identifiers: LCCN 2019032441 (print)
LCCN 2019032442 (ebook)
ISBN 9781645272083 (hardcover)
ISBN 9781645272090 (paperback)
ISBN 9781645272106 (ebook)
Subjects: LCSH: Anger in children—Juvenile literature.
Anger—Juvenile literature.
Classification: LCC BF723.A4 M67 2020 (print)
LCC BF723.A4 (ebook) | DDC 152.4/7—dc23
LC record available at https://lccn.loc.gov/2019032441
LC ebook record available at https://lccn.loc.gov/2019032442

Editor: Susanne Bushman
Designer: Molly Ballanger

Photo Credits: Pete Pahham/Shutterstock, cover; Laboo Studio/Shutterstock, 1; Viktoriia Hnatiuk/Shutterstock, 3; castillodominici/iStock, 4; PicturePartners/iStock, 5 (foreground); Rawpixel.com/Shutterstock, 5 (background); Marta Nardini/Getty, 6–7; Panther Media GmbH/Alamy, 8–9; zhengzaishuru/Shutterstock, 10; Figure8Photos/iStock, 11; Maxim Krivonos/Shutterstock, 12–13; -art-siberia-/iStock, 14; Tassii/iStock, 15; interstid/Shutterstock, 16–17; JGI/Jamie Grill/Blend Images/SuperStock, 18–19; kali9/iStock, 20–21.

Printed in the United States of America at Corporate Graphics in North Mankato, Minnesota.